Bullies and Blacklegs

BRENDA WYN JONES

Gwasg
Gwynedd

First published — July 2002

Text ©: Brenda Wyn Jones 2002
Illustrations ©: Jac Jones 2002

ISBN 0 86074 187 7

Bullies and Blacklegs was originally published as
Bwli a Bradwr by Gwasg Gwynedd in 1998.

Supported by the Arts Council of Wales

*Published and printed
by Gwasg Gwynedd, Caernarfon*

FOR
ELLEN

Before you begin this story...

- The children in this book lived over a hundred years ago in Bethesda, North Wales.

- Their story is told in the old school log books, the diaries where the headteachers recorded the daily life of their school.

- In those days most of the local men worked in the Penrhyn Slate Quarry, producing slate to be sold all over the world.

- Working conditions in the slate industry were poor and the wages low. When the quarrymen protested by calling a strike in November 1900, no-one dreamed that this would be the longest strike in history, lasting for three years.

- Families suffered, especially as time went on, because they were so poor.

- When the owner, Lord Penrhyn, decided to re-open his quarry in June 1901, a few men broke the strike and went back to work. These blacklegs were called 'traitors'.

- From then on there was much bad feeling between the 'traitors' and the strikers, especially as more and more men returned to the quarry.

- The children were affected too by what happened around them, as the log books tell us.

- Welsh was the natural language of their homes and of all village life, but in school English was the only language allowed. The characters tell their story in Welsh, but when they have to speak English, this is shown in italics.

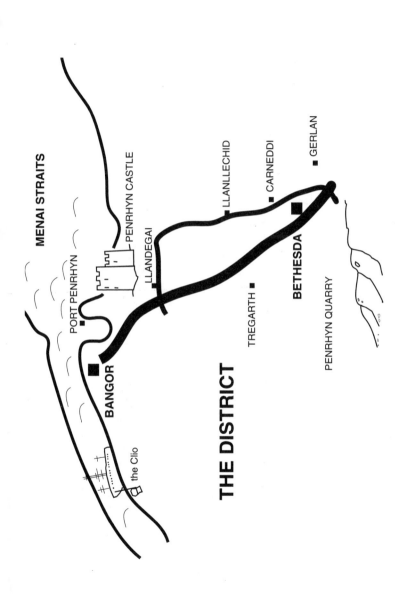

MENAI STRAITS

PORT PENRHYN

PENRHYN CASTLE

BANGOR

the Clio

LLANDEGAI

LLANLLECHID

CARNEDDI

GERLAN

TREGARTH

BETHESDA

PENRHYN QUARRY

THE DISTRICT

THE SCHOOLS

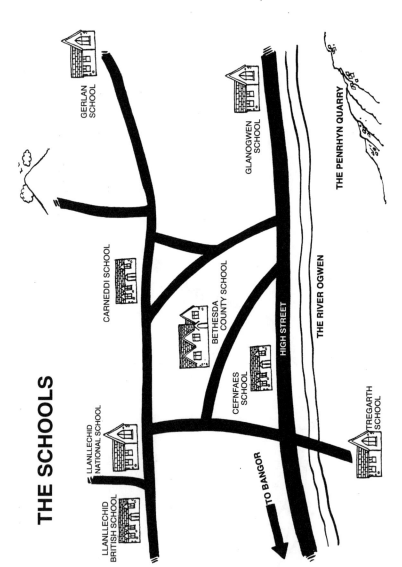

GERLAN SCHOOL

GLANOGWEN SCHOOL

CARNEDDI SCHOOL

LLANLLECHID NATIONAL SCHOOL

LLANLLECHID BRITISH SCHOOL

BETHESDA COUNTY SCHOOL

CEFNFAES SCHOOL

TREGARTH SCHOOL

HIGH STREET

THE RIVER OGWEN

THE PENRHYN QUARRY

TO BANGOR

Chapter 1

Monday, 5 November, 1900

The disturbance in the Quarry has affected the school...

(*Carneddi British School log book – 6 November, 1900*)

> 'Who's going to ja-ail?
>   Who's going to ja-ail?
>   Guto's brothers!
> Jailbirds! Jailbirds!'

Guto cowered against the wall to avoid the bully's fists and prayed for playtime to end. As he listened in vain for the clang of the school bell, Robat and his gang kept on and on with their chanting. They knew that the headmaster was safely out of sight in the kitchen at the back of the school, along with Miss Thomas and the four pupil teachers.

'Stop it!' shouted Davy at last. 'Guto hasn't done anything to you.'

'Oh, but his brothers have, haven't they?' jeered Robat. 'They beat up our Tom and Wil. And my Dad too. You watch – they'll be sent to prison tomorrow. And good riddance too!'

'It must be serious, lads,' added John Edwin. 'There are hundreds of soldiers in Bangor already, in case there's trouble tomorrow.'

'Of course it's serious,' barked Robat. 'No-one had a right to treat Lord Penrhyn's stewards like they did. After all, he owns the quarry. The people of Bethesda are lucky to get work there and they'd all better remember that.'

'But my Dad says it's about time somebody did something about the way they're being treated.'

Good old Davy, thought Guto. He was brave enough to speak up although he too, like everyone else, was afraid of Robat and his cronies.

'It's fine for some of the quarrymen,' Davy went on. 'Those who go to church, not chapel. They're Lord Penrhyn's favourites because they vote for him in every election and support him when there's any trouble in the quarry.' He knew that Robat's family were regular churchgoers.

'But have you heard what they're planning to do tomorrow?' the bully was at it again. 'Some of them are going to march down to the courthouse in Bangor. I hope they get arrested too. It'll serve them right!'

'Well, I'd be with them like a shot if only Mam would let me,' Davy insisted.

'Will you be going, Guto? To see your big brothers being marched off to jail?' Robat laughed scornfully, aiming another cruel punch.

★ ★ ★

'What's going on here?' Mr. Pugh's voice came like a clap of thunder and the crowd around Guto disappeared like magic.

'Get into lines!' he shouted, and everyone knew that he was in a bad mood. They all rushed to their places, dreading to be the last one in case they were

13

punished. Everyone except Guto. He stayed huddled against the wall, breathing heavily and trying his best not to be sick.

'*Come here, boy!*' ordered Mr. Pugh. '*What's wrong with you?*'

'*Nothing, sir,*' whispered Guto, but the headmaster knew that something was going on the moment he saw the children all crowded together in one corner of the yard. He noticed that Griffith Jones looked paler than usual, though the boy never looked very healthy. Then he remembered the court case in

Bangor the following morning and started putting two and two together. One look at the smirk on Robert Hughes's face was enough to convince him that he was right.

'*What's the matter, Griffith?*' he asked, more kindly this time.

'*I… don't feel well, sir.*' Guto had to struggle to find the right words, because school was the only place where they had to speak English. He swallowed hard and tried to stand up straight.

'*Would you like to go to the kitchen to get a drink of water?*'

'*No, thank you, sir.*' Guto squared his shoulders and followed the others into the classroom.

'Are you sure you're alright?' whispered his cousin Maggie as he passed the front desk where she sat in the Big Room. Having seen and heard everything that went on in the yard, she was very worried about him. 'That Robat is an old bully and he's got his knife into you good and proper. Why don't you tell Wil and Llew? They'll soon settle him, you'll see.'

'No, they've got enough to worry about as it is,' muttered Guto, making his way painfully up the steps to his seat behind her. He longed for his fourteenth birthday, when he could leave Carneddi British School for ever and go to work in the quarry. His two big brothers would be there to look after him and he would be free from Robat's bullying at last. But he had almost two long years to wait for that happy day. Although Mr. Pugh had suggested that he sit the Scholarship examination to go to the new County School, he knew that his mother couldn't afford to keep him there.

He picked up his slate and looked across at the blackboard where the headmaster was writing sums for them to copy and work out. But he couldn't concentrate. His mind kept wandering to Bangor and the court case. What if Wil and Llew were sent to prison? What would happen to him and Mam then? It was difficult enough to make ends meet with both his brothers working, because their wages were so low. But without a single penny coming into the house they would starve, or be forced to go on the parish. God help them if it came to that!

He pulled his rag from his pocket and spat on it to wipe his slate clean. As he stared at the date on the blackboard in Mr. Pugh's beautiful handwriting – *November 5th, 1900* – he thought, not for the first time, how odd it looked. Although it was now almost a year since the beginning of the new century, it still felt strange to be writing the year 1900. He had been so used to writing 189– all his life. Then Robat, on his way past his desk to have his work marked, hissed, 'You wait till dinner time. I'll get you then!'

With the pain in his belly, the worry about tomorrow's court case and Robat's threats, Guto felt as sick as a dog. Although he did his best to concentrate on his work, the sound of the quarry hooter from the other side of the valley only made him feel worse. It meant that it was dinner time and that he would have to face Robat and his gang on his way home and back again. He thought of telling his mother that he didn't feel well, and that would be no lie, but she had enough worries already. Although he was close to tears, he was determined not to give Robat any more reason to make fun of him. So he bit his lip and tried to put on a brave face.

Chapter 2

Turbulent quarry affairs affect the attendance.

(Gerlan National School log book – 5 November, 1900)

Guto lay in bed that night, too worried to sleep. He could hear his two brothers snoring in the big bed beside him. How on earth could they sleep so soundly, knowing what they had to face in the morning? Was his mother asleep in the small bedroom downstairs, he wondered? How he would love to creep down the stairs, as he used to when he was a little boy, and cuddle up in the feather bed beside her. He could still remember what a comfort that used to be after waking up from a bad dream.

Robat had had no chance to bully him again that day, thank goodness. He managed to avoid him at dinner time by running all the way home. Then he stayed in the house until he heard the school bell before running all the way back again. Luckily Mr. Pugh kept Robat behind after school, to help him to put the books away and mix more ink. Had the headmaster suspected something? Guto guessed that he knew exactly what was going on and hoped that he would keep an eye on the bully from now on. But I'll still have to face Robat in the morning before school, he thought, and things will be worse than ever because of the court case. Blast the trouble in the quarry, he used to leave me alone before all that started.

His mind wandered back to that terrible day, only a week before. It was morning playtime and all the children were out in the school yard. Suddenly they could hear the clatter of hobnailed boots in the distance, coming nearer and nearer, louder and louder. Everyone rushed to the wall to look down into the road. A crowd of young men were marching past, looking grim and determined. But why? It was only half past ten in the morning! Had there been an accident in the quarry? Oh, no! Not again! Were Wil and Llew safe? What if a slab of slate had fallen from the rock face and killed them? That was how their father had died, although Guto was too young to remember that sad time. Whenever there was a fatal accident in the quarry they stopped work for the rest of the day, out of respect for the dead man and his family.

Then he caught sight of his two brothers marching past. Thank God, they were both safe. But who on earth was the man walking between them with blood all over his face? Had he had an accident? Then why were they marching him home like this? He saw another two being pushed along

further down the line. They looked very frightened and their faces were covered in blood too. What on earth was going on?

'Hey, Wil! What's happened?' he shouted.

'You'll know soon enough, my lad,' came a voice from the crowd, but his brothers marched past without even looking up at him.

* * *

At dinner time all Guto's questions were answered at last. He found his mother in her rocking chair by the fire, crying. Wil, his eldest brother, sat at the table with his head in his hands.

'More and more trouble!' his mother complained. 'How could you treat Richard Hughes and his two boys so cruelly? I won't be able to face people in the village after this. What would your poor father have to say if he were alive today?'

'But Mam fach, we had no choice. Somebody had to do something,' pleaded Wil.

'But why you two? You're always such good boys and you know that Guto and I depend on you. What came over you?'

'We weren't the only ones. There was a crowd of us there when the manager, that Mr. Young, announced that the work will be given out to contractors from now on. That means that we'll all have to work for them. There he was, looking down

his nose at us as if we were dirt. You'd think it was a
privilege to work in his old quarry.'

'But that's how it's always been. Why today of all
days?'

'Because we've all had enough, that's why! We
work fewer and fewer hours, for less and less money,
and they won't let us belong to a trade union. It's
been like this for years now, ever since the Old Lord
died.'

'Yes, the Old Lord was a proper gentleman,' she
sighed. 'Your father had a lot of respect for him.'

'Well, I can tell you this. We don't think much of
his son,' said Wil bitterly. 'All he's interested in is
making more and more money and he treats us like

slaves. But he's gone too far today. Contractors, I ask you! Imagine having to work for people like that Richard Hughes. He's no craftsman, but he knows how to lick Mr. Young's boots by carrying tales to the quarry stewards. Somebody had to make a stand, but the older men with families are afraid of losing their jobs.'

'So it was a crowd of stupid young lads like you who attacked him and his two sons?'

'Yes,' confessed Wil sadly. 'But we had no choice, Mam. Honest!'

'What's happened? Have you been fighting in the quarry?' ventured Guto at last. 'Who were those men covered in blood? Robat Hughes's father and brothers?'

'Go out to play, there's a good boy,' sighed his mother. 'You'll find a piece of bread and dripping on the table in the back kitchen, but heaven knows what we'll have for quarry supper tonight. I can't face going down to the shop, I'm too ashamed.'

'Don't talk nonsense, Mam.' Wil was angry now and Guto escaped through the back door with his dinner in his hand, to look for his other brother. Perhaps he would learn more from him without his mother there, listening to every word.

That was the beginning of all my troubles, he thought sadly, tossing and turning in the lumpy feather bed. He remembered going back to school after dinner on that terrible day and having to face

Robat and his cronies. They were there waiting for him by the school gates and from then on he hadn't had a minute's peace. Unfortunately for him, no-one else in their school had a big brother at the centre of the trouble. And although Davy and some of the other lads were still his friends, they were all afraid of the bully.

It'll be far worse for me in school tomorrow because of the court case in Bangor, he said to himself. He could still see his mother's shocked face that evening when Sergeant Owen came knocking at their door with a summons for his two brothers. But Wil and Llew didn't look very worried when they were asked to report to the police station in the village early next morning. And when he heard that there would be twenty six of them before the court, he knew that many other families in the district were facing the same trouble. Their neighbours had been very kind to them too. He felt better as he remembered all this, but dawn was already breaking when he went to sleep at last.

Chapter 3

The quarrymen en bloc went down this morning to Bangor to accompany the men who had warrants. Very few present in the morning. Dismissed at 11 am and broke up for the afternoon.

(*Carneddi British School log book – 6 November, 1900*)

'Do I have to go to school today, Mam?' asked Guto hopefully at breakfast next morning. 'Hadn't I better stay at home to keep you company?'

He could see his two brothers winking at each other on the opposite side of the table. It was strange seeing them dressed in their Sunday best on a working day. They were both very quiet and that was unusual too. His mother sighed as she stirred the porridge in the big saucepan on the open coal fire.

'No, you'd better go to school as usual, Guto bach. I'll be alright, you'll see.'

'Can't I go to Bangor with Wil and Llew then?'

'Good heavens, no! Don't you dare go near the

place. I've got enough worries with these two, without you getting into trouble as well.'

'But Mam…'

'You listen to Mam now,' said Llew. 'We'll be fine, you'll see.'

'Of course we will,' added Wil. 'We didn't do anything wrong, you know. We were just supporting the other lads.'

'Nothing wrong, indeed!' His mother looked cross as she ladled the hot porridge into the bowls. She went on and on as they ate and in the end Guto was glad of any excuse to leave the table, even though he would have to face Robat when he got to school.

★ ★ ★

'Are you coming to Bangor?' asked Davy as they walked down the hill together.

'No chance,' said Guto sadly. 'Mam would kill me.'

'I suppose we'd better go to school then?'

'Yes, hurry up or we'll be late.'

There were very few children in the yard that morning, although it was nearly nine o'clock. Guto glanced around nervously to see if Robat had arrived yet. Yes, there he was, standing in the far corner with two of his mates, obviously planning something from the furtive looks they gave him. Oh, well, he had more serious problems on his mind now, with his brothers on their way to court. Then he noticed the headmaster standing at the door, watching them like a hawk and missing nothing. Thank goodness, thought Guto. I never dreamt I'd be glad to see him!

By playtime it was obvious that most of the children had stayed away and Mr. Pugh went across to the Infants class to have a word with Miss Thomas. When he came back he called for attention, saying that he had an important announcement to make.

'As you can see, a number of your fellow pupils are absent today, for some reason best known to themselves. School is dismissed for the rest of the day.'

Davy nudged Guto and whispered, 'It's Bangor for us then.'

'David John Williams, were you talking?'

'No, sir.'

'I'm very glad to hear it, or you'd be in detention until dinner time. Now you're to go straight home, all of you. And I want to see you in school at nine o'clock sharp tomorrow morning. Understood?'

'Yessir,' and everyone marched out row by row.

Once again Mr. Pugh kept Robat's row until the very last. By the time they came out of the building, Davy and Guto had disappeared and were running full pelt down the hill to the main road.

'Are you coming now then?'

'I don't know.'

'Oh, come on. No-one will know. You can tell your Mam that we went up the mountain to play.'

'Yes, but what if someone sees us?'

'Don't be stupid. There'll be hundreds of people in Bangor today. And we won't see anyone we know on the way down there either. My Dad said that they were planning to leave the quarry at eight o'clock this morning, so they'll all be in Bangor by now.'

'Oh, alright then. I'll come.'

★ ★ ★

It was such an eerie feeling, walking down the High Street in Bethesda past all the empty shops.

Everywhere was so quiet, it felt exactly like a Sunday.

'How much further?' moaned Davy when they reached the old turnpike, about two miles down the road.

'Come on, hurry up. You were the one who wanted to go and we're not half way there yet.' Then they heard a new sound. They both turned to see a horse and cart coming towards them.

'Whoa, Mari fach.' The farmer pulled on the reins to stop for a chat. 'Hello, lads. Where are you off to?'

'Bangor.'

'Well, hop in then, you're in luck. I'm on my way down to the quay with this load of potatoes. You won't have far to walk to town from there.'

'Great, thanks.' They scrambled aboard and settled down happily among the sacks of potatoes in the cart.

'Are you hungry?' asked the farmer after a while.

'Yes, rather.'

'Well, there's a basket of apples in that corner. Help yourselves.'

'Oh, thanks.'

'And stuff some into your trouser pockets for later on.'

They felt like lords, travelling in comfort and munching happily while the horse trotted obediently along the hard earth road. Now and then the wheels went over a stone or into a pothole and they lurched to one side, laughing. It was all part of the fun.

'Are you going to the courthouse?' asked the farmer when they reached the road to the quay.

'Yes.'

'Well, here you are then, this is where I turn off. Down you get, and you behave yourselves now.'

'Oh, we will. Thank you very much.'

Chapter 4

In consequence of some disturbance in the Quarry this morning, all the men returned about eight o'clock to march in procession to Bangor. The greater part of the children followed them and I was obliged to close school for the day.

(*Tregarth National School log book – November, 1900*)

After saying goodbye to the kind farmer the boys still had half a mile to walk to the courthouse near the town centre, but they could see the crowd long before they reached it.

'Gosh, there must be thousands here!' said Davy as they joined the sea of people stretching out before them.

'Can you see anybody we know?' whispered Guto anxiously.

'Don't be a fool. Nobody will recognize us in this lot. Come on, let's try and get nearer.'

The two edged their way to the front and stared open-mouthed at the soldiers standing in a line guarding the court entrance, each one in his red jacket with his rifle at his side. Then they felt a strange silence all around them – everyone standing quietly, no-one saying a word. The soldiers looked uneasy, eyeing each other and grasping their rifles more tightly, as if they were expecting trouble.

Then a voice came from somewhere in the crowd. One of the men had started to sing and others joined in, one by one: 'Oh, Lord of all Creation, and Saviour of mankind...' Guto knew the hymn well, they often sang it in chapel on a Sunday, but singing was the last thing he felt like doing. He tried to swallow the huge lump in his throat as he thought of poor Wil and Llew somewhere inside that terrible building.

By this time the soldiers were looking even more puzzled, staring at the sea of faces as if they couldn't understand what on earth was going on. The singing rose in the air, wave after wave, growing to a loud crescendo as more and more people joined in. Then suddenly someone shouted: 'They're coming out!' A hush fell on the crowd again, turning into a sigh of relief as they realised that all the men had been set free. The people who were standing in front of Guto and Davy stepped aside to open a path and everyone started clapping and shouting 'hooray'. Then they walked past, Wil and Llew and all the others, smiling happily and looking very relieved.

Thank God! They haven't been sent to jail after

all, was the first thought that raced through Guto's mind as he stood on tiptoe to catch a glimpse of them. Then he suddenly remembered that he wasn't supposed to be there at all and ducked down behind a very tall man.

'Hooray!' shouted Davy. 'They've all been set free!'

'Pipe down, won't you?' whispered Guto. He was furious with his friend for drawing attention to them like this, because he felt sure that Wil had turned round and recognised him. 'I'll be in dead trouble now,' he complained. 'If Wil saw me he's bound to tell Mam.'

★   ★   ★

On their way home the two were careful to keep well away from the quarrymen, but as they were passing the entrance to Penrhyn Castle, where Lord Penrhyn lived in his magnificent home near the village of Llandegai, Davy's father happened to look back and caught a glimpse of them.

'So you came after all, you little rascal,' was all he said to his son. 'Ah, well! It's only right that you should know what's going on.'

'What happened, Dad? Is it all over?'

'No, not by a long way I'm afraid. They were set free because their names had been mixed up, but they all had to pay a shilling for the privilege. And they've got to go back to court again next week.'

'Oh, no!' Guto's heart sank to his boots. He had been so happy when he heard the crowd shouting 'hooray' outside the courthouse.

'Don't you worry, Guto bach,' Davy's father tried to comfort him when he saw the worried look on his thin, pale face. 'Wil and Llew will be fine, you'll see. They say that Lloyd George himself is coming to Caernarfon to defend them next week.'

Guto knew the name of the famous lawyer and Member of Parliament. The words gave him some comfort, but he was still worried about his own fate.

'You won't tell anyone you saw me, will you? If Mam finds out, she'll kill me.'

'No, I won't breathe a word, I promise. But I expect she'll be so glad to see Wil and Llew back home safe and sound, she'll be ready to forgive you anything tonight.'

Guto smiled. You don't know my Mam, he said to himself.

It was great walking with the huge crowd all the way back to Bethesda, especially as it was now beginning to get dark. Guto and Davy felt really grown up, but when they reached the village at last the procession suddenly came to a halt.

'What's happening now I wonder?'

Then the news came back along the lines.

'It's Sergeant Owen with bad news. Lord Penrhyn has decided to close the quarry for a fortnight. To punish us all for leaving today without his permission.'

'Oh, no! This is where the real trouble starts,' said Davy's father, shaking his head sadly. And he never spoke a truer word.

Chapter 5

The attendance this week dropped down considerably, owing to troublesome affairs in the Quarry.

(Gerlan National School log book – 9 November, 1900)

It was still only half past eight, but Davy ran all the way down the hill as if he was going to be late for school. He was dying to have a chat with Guto, to hear how he got on the night before. Had his mother given him a thrashing for going to Bangor, he wondered? Llew came to answer the door when he knocked, looking very worried.

'Is Guto ready?'

'No, and I'm afraid he won't be coming to school today. Will you tell the headmaster that he's ill?'

'Yes, of course. But what's wrong with him? Is he very ill?'

'I'm afraid so, Davy bach. We've had to send for the doctor. Wil is going to the surgery on his way back from the quarry, to ask Doctor Griffiths to call.'

Davy knew only too well why the men had to go to the quarry that morning.

'My Dad's gone there too,' he said. 'To collect his tools.'

'Yes, they all have, but Wil is bringing mine so that I can stay here with Mam and Guto.'

'Tell him I hope he's better soon,' and Davy turned to go.

He must be really bad, he said to himself as he walked slowly down the hill. At first he thought that his friend was only pretending to be ill, to avoid facing Robat after what had happened yesterday. But when he saw the worried look on Llew's face and heard that they were sending for the doctor, he knew that it must be really serious. No-one sent for him unless they were very ill, because it cost so much. I hope it isn't that terrible scarlet fever, he thought, remembering that two children from their school had died of the disease the year before.

'Where's your mate today?' shouted Robat spitefully when he caught sight of Davy walking in through the school gates. 'Too scared to come to school is he? What a shame. We were going to give him a really warm welcome today, weren't we, lads?'

Davy walked on, keeping his head down and his hands in his pockets. His fists were clenched tightly, but he was wise enough to keep his feelings to himself. He knew that the bully would love any

excuse to start a fight and then put the blame on someone else.

* * *

'Since when has the boy been ill?' Doctor Griffiths peered over his spectacles at Guto while he felt his pulse.

'Last night, Doctor. I woke up in the early hours and heard him tossing and turning in the bedroom above me. He was hot all over and sweating like a pig and he's been like that ever since. His eyes are troubling him too, they're so red and sore.'

'Hmm… yes. Let me listen to your chest, young man,' said the doctor cheerfully, lifting the bedclothes and then Guto's nightshirt.

'Goodness me! How did you get all these bruises?' he asked in surprise.

'I fell,' lied Guto as he hurriedly pulled his nightshirt down to hide the black marks before his mother could get a good look at them.

'You fell, did you? I see. Now sit up so that I can have a closer look at your eyes.'

He looked intently into Guto's face for a long time and then stood up.

'Well, Mrs. Jones, I'm afraid he'll have to stay in bed for a week at least. It's important that he drinks enough and keeps warm, in case the fever turns into pneumonia or worse. And I'll get you some ointment for his eyes.'

'Oh, thank you, Doctor,' said his mother gratefully. 'I'll make sure he stays in bed until you come again.' On his way down to the village the doctor called at Carneddi school to have a word with the headmaster.

Chapter 6

Thursday, 22 November, 1900

A considerable drop in the weekly attendance figures, from 317 to 292. Several children are suffering from inflammation of the eyes, but many are taking advantage of the Lock-Out in the Quarry.

(Carneddi British School log book – 7 December, 1900)

'Are you feeling better?'

At last Davy had been allowed to see his friend. He tried not to stare at him lying there on the couch by the window with his mother's shawl over his shoulders, looking so frail and ill. The curtains were drawn, as if someone in the house had died, and the kitchen looked different in the dim light. Guto's eyes must still be troubling him, thought Davy, like many of the other children in school by now.

'I've been dying to see you. Do you realise that it's over a fortnight since our trip to Bangor? What happened to you? Did you get a thrashing when you got home?'

'No, I was lucky. Wil and Llew saw me creeping into the house through the back door and said that I'd been with them.'

'You had a lucky escape, then.'

'You're right. Mam was reaching for the birch rod the minute she saw me. She'd been worrying about me all day, once she heard that school was closed.'

Davy turned to look at the birch rod hanging on two nails above the fireplace and gave a sigh of relief. He was glad his own parents didn't believe in having such a thing in the house, but of course he had a father to put him across his knee when he misbehaved.

'When are you coming back to school then?'

'I'm not sure. Next Monday perhaps, but I have to see the doctor first.'

'I'm looking forward to having you back, I can tell you.'

'I'm not, I hate the thought of it,' confessed Guto. 'Is Robat still throwing his weight around?'

'No, he's been very quiet since you've been away. Pugh gave him a real telling-off for something, but nobody knows what.'

'Oh, he'll be at it again next week, you'll see. As soon as he catches sight of me,' sighed Guto.

'Don't you worry. I'll be there to look after you. But why don't you tell Wil and Llew about him?' suggested Davy.

'No, I don't want to cause them any more trouble. They've got enough worries as it is.'

'But they weren't sent to jail were they? And all the men have gone back to work today. Wasn't it a shame we couldn't go to the second court case in Caernarfon?'

'Didn't you go?'

'No, I didn't feel like going by myself when you were so ill.'

'I wonder what happened?'

'Don't you know?'

'No, nobody ever tells me anything in this house. All I know is that Wil and Llew were set free, thank God.'

'Well, six of the other lads were sent to jail for three months.'

'Never! Who were they?'

'Two from this village, but I don't know the other four.'

'That's terrible.'

'Yes, I know. Pugh sent us home that day too, because only a handful of us turned up.'

'And why is school closed today?'

'It isn't.'

'Why aren't you there, then?'

'I've got some shopping to do for Mam in the village.'

★ ★ ★

The next moment the front door opened and Wil and Llew stormed in. The two boys looked up at them in surprise, sensing that something dreadful had happened in the quarry that morning.

'What's wrong?' Guto was the first to speak. 'Has there been an accident?'

'No.' Llew sat down wearily, throwing his bag on the table. 'We're on strike!'

'Strike?' They'd heard the dreaded word many times as they listened to the grown ups discussing the 1896 strike, but they were both too young to remember much about it.

'What are you two doing here at this time of day?' Guto's mother walked in and stood in the middle of the kitchen floor with a load of firewood in her arms. Wil and Llew looked at each other guiltily, each hoping the other would be brave enough to tell her the bad news.

'We're on strike, Mam,' confessed Llew at last.

'Strike? Oh, no! You've only just gone back to work...'

'Yes, and when we got there the manager sacked eight hundred of us.'

'Eight hundred? But only a handful of you young ones caused all this trouble. I was afraid that you two wouldn't get your jobs back today, I must confess. But eight hundred? Why would Lord Penrhyn do such a terrible thing?'

'Oh, he's just showing us who's the boss,' said Wil bitterly. 'But we'll show him yet.'

'All the men agreed to call a strike. We've got to let him know once and for all that he can't treat us like this,' added Llew.

'But another strike?' His mother remembered how poor they had been four years before when the men were out for almost a year. It had all been so pointless because in the end they had to go back to work on Lord Penrhyn's terms. She walked slowly towards the grate, opened the small cupboard beside the fire and put the firewood in it to dry. Then she grabbed the poker to prod the fire and sat in her rocking chair, staring into the flames and shaking her head sadly. No-one said a word for a long time and Davy was beginning to feel uncomfortable, sitting there in silence listening to the grandfather clock in the corner slowly ticking away.

'Well, I'd better be off,' he said at last. 'Mam wants a few things from the shop. I'll call again to see you, Guto.'

'Yes, you'd better go, Davy bach. She'll be waiting for you and I expect your father will be home by now.'

'Yes, you're right.' Davy wondered what his own mother would say when she heard that the quarrymen were out on strike once again.

Chapter 7

Most of the writing was done on slates this week as the weather was extremely cold.

(*Tregarth National School log book – 11 January, 1901*)

'Looking forward to school today, Guto?' asked Wil as they sat eating their breakfast on the first Monday of the new year. He was watching his young brother playing with his porridge instead of eating it, twirling it round and round the plate with his spoon.

Guto hadn't been sent back to school before Christmas after all. Because of his bad cough his mother had decided to keep him home until the New Year. Christmas was a dismal one that year, with money being so short, and all they could afford for dinner on the day itself was a tough old hen which had to be boiled before being roasted. But at last school was re-opening after the holidays and Guto had to steel himself to face Robat once again.

'Why don't you answer your brother?' His mother was cross with him for staring at his plate without saying a word. 'Come on now, eat your breakfast like a good boy or you'll never get your strength back. You're looking forward to going back to school I hope?'

'Yes and no,' said Guto miserably.

'What kind of an answer is that?' His mother still sounded cross.

'There's something worrying you, isn't there?' Llew looked concerned.

'No, nothing!' And Guto missed a golden opportunity to tell them about the big black cloud that had been hanging over him for the last two months.

'The trouble with you, my lad, is that you're beginning to enjoy being at home,' scolded his mother. 'But you're much better now. Just remember to wrap up warm, it's bitterly cold outside and I'm afraid there's more snow on the way.'

'Wouldn't it be better if I waited one more week then, Mam? The classroom will be damp and cold after the holidays and I don't want to catch another cold, do I?'

'Nonsense! You can wear your thickest jumper and your best Sunday boots. It'll do you the world of good to go out for a change.' His mother was determined to send him back before he became too fond of being at home all day with his brothers. He could see the two of them winking at each other and trying hard to keep a straight face.

'Alright then. See you at dinner time,' he sighed as he stood up to fetch his outdoor clothes.

★　★　★

'Don't worry. I'm here to look after you.'

As they walked down the hill, Davy noticed that his friend was looking nervous and that his eyes were still red and sore. He felt really sorry for him.

'Robat isn't half as popular as he used to be, you know,' he tried to comfort him. 'His father's on strike too, just like the rest of us.'

When they reached the school gates a crowd of boys came rushing straight at them and Guto's heart leapt to his mouth. He stared wildly about him, but there was no sign of Robat among them.

'Are you better, Guto?'

'Gosh, you've been ill for a long time.'

'You still look a bit pale.'

'Never mind, you'll soon get better.'

'Look, I had this new ball for Christmas. Fancy a game?'

Guto was overwhelmed by such a warm welcome. After all, some of these used to be Robat's friends and most of the others had been too afraid to stand up to him.

'I told you everything would be alright, didn't I?' smiled Davy, and indeed there was no sign of the bully anywhere, not even after the bell. Guto began to feel much happier. Was his old enemy ill, he wondered? So ill that he might even die? That would solve all his problems!

While these pleasant thoughts drifted through his mind, the headmaster's harsh voice shattered his daydreams. As he marched in through the door and into the classroom with the others, the big dark room felt cold and damp, even though the coal fire in the grate was doing its best. They all stood in silence, waiting for Mr. Pugh to appear. When he came at last, Robat and John Edwin were with him and Guto's heart sank.

'You only just made it in time, boys.' The headmaster looked very cross. *'Another few seconds and both of you would have earned a late mark. Where have you been?'*

'Down to the shop, sir. A message for my mother,' gasped Robat. He was panting and looked as if he had run all the way to school.

'Errand, boy – errand. And what about you, John Edwin Pritchard? Another errand?'

'No, sir. I went with Robert for company.'

'Company, indeed! Well, you can both stay in and keep each other company during morning playtime. To your places, at once!'

I'm safe for the time being, Guto comforted himself as he watched them walking with their heads down to their places at the bench. With luck he might be able to sneak home at dinner time, too. He just had to hope for the best.

★   ★   ★

Guto enjoyed running around and kicking the ball with the other lads at playtime after sitting still for such a long time. His hands felt like two blocks of ice after holding the cold slate to do his sums. Usually they could look forward to writing in ink in their exercise books in the Composition lesson before dinner, but not that morning, unfortunately. The ink had frozen in the little china ink wells in their holes in the benches.

It was such a relief to be free, without having to glance over his shoulder every other second. Everyone seemed so friendly too, it was almost like old times except for a small group of Robat's close friends. They refused to join in the game, but stood in a huddle at the far end of the yard.

Then Guto suddenly realised that he was dying to go to the toilet.

'Can't you wait until dinner time?' shouted Davy. He was determined to play on until it was time for the bell.

'No, I have to go now.' Between all the worry and excitement of the morning and the cold weather, Guto was desperate. He ran to the smelly lavatories at the back of the school, leaving Davy and the others kicking the ball around the yard.

A few minutes later, as he walked back out through the door, who should he come face to face with but Robat. It was such a shock, especially when he had been so sure that he was safe for the time being. He stood his ground bravely, but he felt as weak as a kitten.

'Oh, and how's the big baby then? Still being nursed by his mammy, eh? And where are your brothers today? I'll tell you where they should be – in jail with the others! I've waited a long time for this, and when I've finished with you don't you dare say a word to Pugh. Or you'll get another beating – understand?'

He took one menacing step forward, his fists raised. Guto just stood there and closed his eyes, waiting for the first blow. Then suddenly a gang of boys rushed in and stood like a wall between the two of them. Davy was in charge, he must have seen Robat sneaking out of the school building and realised that his friend was in danger. But there were others there, too. Ben Slate Cottage for one. Guto wasn't surprised to see him, but what about some of the others? These were the lads who usually sided with the bully to save their own skins.

'Well, well, and who have we here?' asked Robat spitefully, although by now he didn't sound so very sure of himself. There wasn't a single one of his own mates in the crowd. 'I don't need your help with this

one, lads. Just stand back and watch me settle him once and for all!'

'Leave him be!' Davy came forward to face him. 'He's suffered enough already and you're not to lay a finger on him ever again, do you hear?'

'Says who?'

'We all do. Don't we, lads?'

'Yes,' agreed the others, surprising Guto even more than the bully himself.

'Oh, I see,' said Robat crossly. Without his cronies around him, he was a real coward, like all bullies.

'So I'm not good enough for you now, am I?' He stared defiantly at his old supporters.

'Just you behave yourself from now on and leave Guto alone. Or we'll all gang up on you, won't we lads?'

'Yes,' chorused everyone once more and Robat had to go back to class with his tail between his legs. But not before making sure that he had the last word, as usual.

'Just you wait. You won't get away with this. You'll see!'

Walking home at the end of that morning, Guto felt happier than he had been for a very long time. He laughed as Davy made fun of Robat, and his rosy cheeks and happy face brought a smile even to his mother's face when she saw him.

'Well, well. I knew that going back to school would do you the world of good, my lad. You're looking so much better.'

'I feel great, Mam,' smiled Guto as he sat down to enjoy his dinner.

Chapter 8

Many families appear to be leaving the neighbourhood and during the last few weeks twelve or fifteen girls have left school.

(Glanogwen National Girls' School log book – 16 March, 1901)

Guto was happier than he had been for a very long time, even though the weather was bitterly cold for the first few weeks of the year. There wasn't enough to eat because they were so poor, but he was slowly getting his strength back after being so ill. The main reason for this was that he was free from Robat's bullying at last, although his old enemy still kept on at him when the other children weren't around. Everyone longed for the spring and the warmer weather so that they could fish in the rivers, gather cockles on the sea shore and bilberries on the hills.

One day in March he came home from school to find his mother sitting in her rocking chair, crying. For a moment he thought that someone had died, but as he stood there quietly, listening to her arguing with Wil and Llew, he realised that it was something quite different. They had decided to go away to look for work.

'But we've got to do something,' pleaded Wil. 'Try to understand, Mam. We can't stand around here doing nothing week after week, with no money coming in to keep us all.'

'But we're all in this trouble together and no-one else has gone so far away.'

'Yes they have,' insisted Llew. 'A few of the lads are already working in Liverpool docks.'

'But that isn't on the other side of the world,' she pleaded.

'Where are you going then?' asked Guto.

His brothers turned to look at him, but neither said a word.

'To America, Guto bach,' said his mother at last, sighing as if the end of the world had come. 'Why on earth they've decided to go so far, I can't imagine. We'll never see them again as long as we live.'

'Don't be silly, Mam.' Wil was beginning to lose his temper. 'We'll be rich in no time, you'll see. Then we'll come home, I promise.'

'We'll send money too,' said Llew. 'The little we get from the Strike Fund isn't half enough and we can't live on bread and dripping for much longer.'

'How will you pay your fares out there? It's going to cost you a fortune.' Guto knew exactly where America was after studying the shiny brown map on the classroom wall and learning about the United States in the Geography lessons. He wondered if Wil and Llew realised what a long way it was to New England, where the slate quarries were.

The two stared at him open mouthed, and then at each other. It was obvious that they hadn't thought of the cost, only of getting to the New World to make their fortunes there. America wasn't mentioned after that, but in less than a week they decided to try their luck in the South Wales coal mines. They had managed to scrounge enough money to pay their train fares and their mother was now quite willing for them to go. She was so relieved when they gave up all thoughts of going to America. And although she still felt that Bridgend, where her cousin Megan lived, was a long way away, at least it was better than going to the other side of the world.

* * *

'Wil and Llew are going down South to look for work,' announced Guto on the way to school the next morning.

'My Dad's thinking of going too,' sighed Davy.

'Why? Don't you want him to? We've got to get money from somewhere, Wil says.'

'Yes, I know all that. But it's bad news for you and me, isn't it?'

'What do you mean?'

'Well, who do you think will have to do all the work around the house when they've gone? Feed the chickens, gather firewood, dig the garden and all the other jobs?'

'Gosh, you're right. I never thought of that. But the Strike can't last for ever, can it? They'll soon be back home, I hope.'

'When are they going then?'

'Tomorrow morning.'

'Let's go down to the station to see them off.'

'No, we can't. They're catching the seven o'clock train. Too early for me, Mam says.'

They walked confidently through the school gates to join all the other children waiting for the bell. There was no need for Guto to worry about Robat any more. The big gang who used to crowd around him had dwindled to two or three at the most – John Edwin and a couple of the other lads who lived in the same street.

Then Guto saw the four of them standing by the wall at the far corner of the yard, looking as if they were hiding something. Suddenly he remembered how he himself used to feel, cowering against that very wall being threatened and punched. It looked very suspicious so he decided to find out what they were doing.

'Look, Davy. He's up to his old tricks again,' he whispered. 'Let's go over to see what's going on.'

'Leave him alone,' was Davy's advice. He didn't want to go looking for trouble.

'But I'm sure he's up to no good,' insisted Guto as he crossed the yard.

He was right too. As he drew nearer he could see a little boy from Standard Three leaning against the wall, sniffing and crying. Robat was obviously enjoying himself.

'Hey, what do you think you're doing?' shouted Guto. 'Stop bullying Ned bach. Let him go.'

'You mind your own business! This one's been asking for it, calling us names and making a nuisance of himself.'

'Oh, so you've started to bully the little ones now, have you? Too scared to tackle us, eh?' Davy had walked over quietly with the other boys and they all took up their positions behind Guto.

'Give him a good hiding, Guto,' shouted someone and suddenly he realised that he would have to do just that if he wanted to settle the bully once and for all. Although he didn't feel like tackling him yet, he rolled up his sleeves and raised his fists, ready to fight. Then he noticed that Robat was looking hopefully at the school door and smiled. He knew exactly what was going through his mind. He's praying for the bell to ring, he thought, just as I used to do.

Mr. Pugh appeared just then, swinging the handbell as he walked across the yard. Thank

goodness! Guto gave a sigh of relief. He didn't want to hurt anyone, not even Robat. He knew from bitter experience what it was like to be bullied. And although he knew that he would have to face his old enemy one day soon, he felt that he wasn't strong enough. Not yet.

Chapter 9

Attendance not so good this week owing partly to the disturbed state of the Quarry.
(Glanogwen National Girls' School log book – 10-14 June, 1901)

'Will you walk home with me this afternoon?' asked Maggie, Guto's cousin. It was afternoon playtime on the first day of school after the Easter holidays. Guto and Davy looked at her in surprise.

'But you must know your own way home by now!' laughed Davy. 'What on earth's the matter with you today? You're not in the Infants class any more, silly.'

'Anyway, we go the other way,' Guto was puzzled. 'You don't expect us to walk to your house and then back again, do you?'

'Well...' Poor Maggie was obviously finding it hard to explain. 'Oh, never mind!' she said at last. 'I can manage.'

Then Guto noticed the troubled look on her face and sensed that there was something seriously wrong. This was so unlike her, because she was such a sensible girl. Although she was only ten years old

61

he knew that she was a great help to her mother, helping her to care for the five younger children in the family.

'Come on,' he said, in a kinder voice. 'Why don't you tell us what's worrying you?'

'Oh, forget it!' she snapped and ran over to join the girls at the other end of the yard.

All through that long afternoon, as he listened to Mr. Pugh going on and on in the history lesson about the great British Empire, Guto found it very hard to concentrate. He kept worrying about Maggie. Eventually he was told off for not paying attention and had to make a real effort to get on with his work, but his mind kept wandering. What on earth could be wrong?

He stared at her, sitting up as stiff as a poker and biting her lip as if she were in pain. Then he happened to notice that Robat, who was sitting higher up on the bench behind her, kept kicking her in the small of her back. She was struggling to remain quite still, in case Mr. Pugh told her off for fidgeting, but she was obviously in pain. Of course! At last he knew the answer. Robat lived quite near her and was bullying her on the way to and from school.

★ ★ ★

'You could be right,' agreed Davy when Guto told him what he'd seen. 'That's exactly what you'd expect from that coward. He daren't bully us any more, so he's starting on the girls now.'

'And picking on her because she's my cousin.' Guto was furious as he thought of this and decided that the time had come for him to settle Robat once and for all. He stood by the door to wait for Maggie.

'There you are at last. Look, we'll walk home with you,' he smiled at her.

'It's that Robat isn't it?' asked Davy.

'Yes,' she confessed. 'He was worse than usual today.'

'I thought he'd learnt his lesson when Guto threatened to give him a hiding. Do you remember? When he started to bully Ned bach?'

Yes, they both remembered that day. Robat had been quiet ever since, because he knew that they weren't afraid of him any more. As for Guto himself, he wanted to forget their old quarrel, especially after Mr. Pugh's warning. He had meant every word of it when he announced that he would expel anyone caught fighting or causing a disturbance in school because of the troubles in the quarry. Although they were ready to face the cane when they misbehaved, this would be a thousand times worse. They all knew that children who were really troublesome were sent to the 'Big Ship'! The old navy training ship, the Clio, lay at anchor in the Menai Straits a few miles away and parents often threatened their children that they would send them there unless they behaved themselves. Being locked in the dark cupboard under the stairs was bad enough, and that had happened to Guto more than once, but he didn't want to face the hard life on the Clio.

'Is it just you, or does he bully the other girls?'

'Yes, we're all afraid of him. Gwen and her sister have stayed home today because they're too scared to come to school.'

'Well, he's asking for it then.' Guto was really angry now.

'But we daren't lay a finger on him, remember,' Davy warned. 'Don't forget the warning Pugh gave us. He meant it too.'

'Yes, you're right. And that little sneak would go straight home to tell his father.'

'And he'd be in school like a shot first thing tomorrow morning to complain to Pugh about us.'

'What can we do, then?'

'We'll see Maggie home first. We're bound to meet him on the way back.'

'Right. Don't worry, we'll soon settle him for you. And we'll make sure he behaves from now on.'

'Oh, thanks!' she sighed with relief. 'But don't you two get into any trouble because of me, will you?'

'Of couse not. He's such a big baby, it'll be easy to scare him. Especially since he knows that we're all ganging up on him now.'

★ ★ ★

There was no sign of the bully all the way to Maggie's home. He must have seen them setting off from school together and stayed behind on purpose. After making sure that she was safe, the two stood at the end of the street for a while in case he turned up.

'I can't wait any longer,' Davy decided after a while. 'Mam will be expecting me to help with the chickens. We'll probably see him on our way back anyway.' They set off towards Carneddi and indeed, as they rounded a bend in the road, who should be coming to meet them but Robat and his mate, John Edwin.

'Look who's here! What a nice surprise!' Robat tried to sound confident, but his friend looked really scared.

'I haven't done anything, honest,' he said as Guto and Davy stood in the middle of the road to challenge them. Then he rushed past, leaving Robat to face them alone.

'Let him go,' called Davy over his shoulder as he stood, feet astride and arms folded. 'This is the one we want to settle today.'

'Well, well. It looks as if you haven't got a single friend left,' mocked Guto.

'What do you want, lads?' Robat wasn't so sure of himself by now.

'You never listen, do you?'

'What do you mean?'

'We warned you over a month ago to behave yourself, or else...'

'But I have, honest. I've left you alone since then, haven't I?'

'Yes, but when we warned you not to bully little boys, what did you do then? Start on the girls.'

'Oh, I see it all now. Maggie's been opening her big mouth, has she?'

'No, she hasn't as it happens. She refused to tell us what was wrong, but I saw you kicking her in the history lesson this afternoon.'

'Just a bit of fun. I didn't realise she was such a cry baby,' said Robat spitefully.

'You're the biggest baby around here, you bully.' Guto was really worked up by now and stood with his hands clenched, ready at last to settle the score. He took a step forward and raised his fists, but Davy grabbed his arm to stop him.

'I think he's learnt his lesson,' he said quietly. 'Now this is your last warning. If you give us any trouble from now on, you'll get such a hiding you won't forget it in a hurry. And we'll warn the other children as well, so everyone will be keeping an eye on you. Understand?'

Robat just stood there with his head down, scraping the dust with the toe of his boot.

'Well, answer us. Do you or don't you?' Guto was shouting now.

'Yes,' he mumbled at last, 'but I'll tell my Dad about you, and Pugh too.'

'Pugh won't listen to your lies,' said Davy. 'He knows you too well. Now off you go home like a good boy, and remember what we said.'

They both stood watching him as he walked away slowly with his hands in his pockets.

'Why didn't you let me give him a good hiding?' Guto was still angry.

'No. He isn't worth it and you'd only get into trouble. I don't think he'll be any bother from now on. Do you?'

Chapter 10

*It was reported that many parents
had withdrawn their children from school
because there are children here whose
fathers have returned to the Quarry.*

(*Llanllechid National School log book – 3-6 September, 1901*)

*A large number of children admitted from
the National School.*

(*Llanllechid British School log book – 6 September, 1901*)

During that summer term Guto had grown tall and strong. Now that Wil and Llew were working down a coal mine in the Rhondda, they were able to send money home regularly. He felt much happier, although he still missed his two brothers. School was better too, now that Robat was no threat to him or to anyone else.

When the summer holidays came at last, Robat went away to work on his uncle's farm up the valley and everyone was much happier without him. Guto was busier than ever, helping the local farmers with the hay and the sheep shearing, and then roaming the hills with Davy to gather bilberries. When the blackberry season arrived they collected huge basketfuls for their mothers to make jam, ready for

the coming winter. Between all this and the work around the house, they were both quite relieved when school started again in September.

As they walked down the hill on that very first day, they were glad to see that every house had a sign in the front window – **NID OES BRADWR YN Y TŶ HWN.** (*No traitors in this house.*) Since early summer a small number of men had sneaked back to the quarry to work, breaking the strike. All the other quarrymen were disgusted with these blacklegs, or 'traitors' as they were called, for letting them down at a time like this.

'Have you heard?' was Davy's first question that morning. 'John Edwin's father has gone back to the quarry.'

'I'm not surprised,' answered Guto. 'They're very friendly with Robat's family, and his father and two brothers were the first to go back.'

'Well, they're in for a warm welcome this morning,' laughed Davy. 'They haven't a single friend left now.'

But there was no sign of either of them in the yard, or in the classroom after the bell. How disappointing, thought Guto, as he stood waiting for the headmaster to arrive. He was eager to see the two of them today, when a year ago it would have been such a relief to know that they weren't going to be there. How things had changed!

When Mr. Pugh walked in through the door, he was followed by three boys and two little girls, looking very shy and unsure of themselves.

'I want you to welcome five new pupils today,' he announced. *'They've transferred here from another school and I want you to help them settle down with us as soon as possible. I know you'll all do your best.'*

'Who are they, I wonder?' whispered Davy.

'I know him, the tallest one,' replied Guto. 'He comes from Llanllechid and his dad used to work with Wil and Llew in the quarry.'

'Why are they coming here, then? Do you think they've moved here to live?'

'No, I don't think so. Or my Mam would have been the first to hear of it.'

'Silence!' Mr. Pugh had found a seat for the three boys at the front bench and sent the two girls to Miss Thomas in the Infants' class. They had to wait until morning playtime before the mystery was solved.

★ ★ ★

'Have you moved here from Llan to live then?' was Davy's first question when Tommy, the eldest of the new boys, came out to play.

'No, we've just changed schools,' was the reply.

'Where were you before?'

'The Church school in Llanllechid.'

'Why have you moved then? It's a long way for you to walk.'

'Yes, you're right, but Llan school is full of traitors. My Dad doesn't want us to mix with them.'

'Why don't you go to the British school in Llan then?'

'Because they're full already. And my parents thought we'd be happier here.'

'Are you all brothers and sisters then?' Davy was still curious.

'Yes, but we're not the only family who feels like this. You wait. A lot more children will be moving here before long.'

'Gosh, your old school will be very empty if that happens,' remarked Guto.

'No, the traitors have started moving their children there from the British school. And we passed two Carneddi boys on their way there this morning. Their fathers have gone back to the quarry too, my Dad said.'

Guto and Davy looked at each other. Of course! Robat and John Edwin! That's why they weren't in school.

'Good riddance too, though it would have been fun to have them here today.' Davy sounded disappointed.

'No,' Guto smiled and shook his head. 'Don't you realise that this is the best news we've ever had? Think for a minute, lads. Why haven't we been able to settle them both long before now? Because Pugh threatened to expel us if we caused any trouble. But if they've left, well…'

'Hey, you're right!' agreed Davy. 'Now we can do what we like with them!'

Chapter 11

The British School children are very troublesome. Today they watched two of our children for the purpose of illtreating them and, when these children were escorted homewards, the master was hooted and called all bad names. The case was reported to the British School master and also to the police.

Not a day has passed since the re-opening after the holidays but that our school children are called after or otherwise illtreated by the children of the British School.

(Llanllechid National School log book – 16 September, 1901.)

Although Guto and his friends searched for Robat and John every evening that week, there was no sign of them anywhere in the village. They must have guessed what was happening and were careful to stay indoors. But they were up to their old tricks again on their way home from school every day, pestering Tommy and his younger brothers and sisters.

'Why don't we walk home with Tommy this afternoon?' Guto suggested to Davy on their way to school on Friday morning. 'We're bound to meet them somewhere along the road.'

'That's a great idea and we'll ask the other lads to come too.'

Everyone agreed at once and Guto began to feel really important. It was great to be the leader of the gang, he thought, as he started giving orders.

'We're bound to see them on their way home and this time we'll be ready for them. Where do you meet them usually, Tommy?'

'About half way home, by the old farm gate.'

'Right. This is what we'll do. We'll hide behind the wall by the gate. Then we can give them the surprise of their lives when they come round the corner.'

'And when we've done that, why don't we go to meet the traitors on their way home from the quarry? Look, I've got this shell and it makes a great hooting noise,' added Davy.

Everyone knew exactly what he meant. For some weeks now the strikers' wives had been using sea shells to hoot at the traitors as they were escorted by the police to and from the quarry. The children thought this was great fun and enjoyed watching the men's faces as they walked past, a few with their heads held high but most of them looking down at the ground in shame.

★ ★ ★

'Hush, they're coming!' Guto and his gang went to hide behind the wall, while Tommy and his brothers and sisters walked slowly along the road.

'How did they treat you in the British School today?'

They could all hear Robat's spiteful voice and were dying to get at him, but Guto raised his hand to stop them. He wanted the two bullies to come near enough for them to jump out and surprise them. But when he heard one of the little girls crying, he knew that they had to act quickly.

'Now!' he ordered and they all leapt out from their hiding place to grab the two before they realised what was happening. When John saw who they were he looked at his friend in terror, expecting him to do something. But Robat knew that it was all up with them. He made one last effort to save his own skin, knowing that Guto and Davy would treat him much more fairly than he himself had ever treated anyone.

'Hey, what's this?' he asked boldly, although his heart was beating like a drum. 'Ten against two? Fair play now, lads.'

'Fair play?' Davy spat out the words. 'Who are you to talk about fair play, you traitor?'

'No, he's quite right,' said Guto quietly. 'It should be one against one, so take this for a start!' He leapt forward suddenly, aiming his fist at Robat's face, and from then on the bully had no chance. Guto had waited a long time for this and he sensed that he was now the stronger of the two. His opponent made one feeble attempt to raise his fists and wave them about wildly, but Guto kept dancing out of his reach and then leaping in with fierce blows – to his body, then his face, then his body again.

Before anyone could count to ten, Robat had had enough. He rushed like a mad bull through the circle, his face covered in blood, with John following him like a little dog. But not before Davy had dealt him a few blows too, to teach him a lesson.

'Just you keep away from Tommy and the others from now on,' Guto shouted after them. 'Or we'll have to give you another dose to remind you.'

'Thanks, lads,' said Tommy happily. 'Come along, you lot. Time we went home.'

Chapter 12

We have had frequent cases of disobedience to the teachers of late...

(Cefnfaes British School log book – 11 October, 1901)

Children from Gerlan attending Carneddi School go round the houses – the homes of the children attending this school – and entreat and persuade our scholars to leave our school.

(Gerlan National School log book – 4 July, 1902)

By the end of that term many more strikers had moved their children to Carneddi school and Guto was now the leader of a much bigger gang. They enjoyed teasing the traitors' children on their way home from the Church schools in Gerlan and Llanllechid every day. Then on Saturday a crowd of them would walk to Gerlan, to try to persuade the strikers' children who were still attending the Church school there to join them in Carneddi.

Although this was a happy and exciting time for

him, he had one big worry. For some strange reason, Davy was not such a close friend as he used to be. He kept making excuses to avoid joining them on these outings and he often looked worried, as if he had something on his mind. When Guto asked him at last what was wrong, he confessed that he was worried about his sister Sally.

'She's very ill,' he explained. 'She's got T.B. and Doctor Griffiths says that she'll need plenty of fresh air and good food if she's going to get better. But what hope has she got, with my Dad on strike? We can't even afford to buy medicine for her or pay the doctor's bills.'

Davy's father hadn't gone away to look for work after all. For one thing, his mother was getting too old to look after herself and he was her only son. Then, when Sally became ill, it was impossible for his wife to care for them both. Guto's mother, like all the other neighbours, did all she could to help, often giving Davy some food to take home on his way from school.

★   ★   ★

Davy looks more worried than ever today, Guto thought one Friday in school. I hope things aren't any worse. Although he was sorry for his friend, he felt disappointed that he hadn't told him about Sally long before now. After all, that's what friends were for and he still remembered how faithful Davy had been when Robat was making life so difficult for him. Here was a chance for him to do something for his old friend in return. He decided to ask him at the end of afternoon school what he could to help, but Davy had disappeared by the time he came out into the yard. That had never happened before and Guto felt very hurt. Things must be much worse today, he thought.

'I think I'll go up to see Davy this morning,' he told his mother the next day.

'You'll do no such thing,' was the answer. 'There's plenty of work around the house to keep you busy until dinner time, then you can come over to Aunty Jinnie's house with me this afternoon. That way I'll know exactly where you are and I won't have to worry about you.'

'Why should you worry about me?'

'Because you're always causing trouble, you and your friends, that's why.'

'But Mam, that isn't true. We're just trying to help the men who are on strike by making life difficult for the traitors' children.'

'That's not what I heard from Pugh the School. Why did he come here to complain about you then? I was so ashamed. You've grown far too big for your boots, my lad, and you've become a real bully too, so Mr. Pugh says. Oh, I wish we could see the end of this old strike so that Wil and Llew could come back home. They'd soon make you see sense. You used to be such a good boy, but now I can't do a thing with you.'

'Pugh had to go to everyone's house, Mam. Because the Llan headmaster complained about us.'

'God knows there's enough trouble and bad feeling in this village without you children adding to it. We'll have to learn to live together again once all this is over. You try to remember that.'

'Can I go to see Davy after tea then?'

'No you can't and that's final. It'll be dark by then and I don't want you troubling them, with Sally fach so ill. You'll see Davy in chapel tomorrow morning. And whatever happens, don't you forget that his family are going through a very difficult time right now.'

'What do you mean, Mam? What's going to happen?' Was Sally going to die, he wondered, and that really frightened him.

'Never you mind. You'll know soon enough, my boy.'

With that Guto had to be content, he couldn't persuade his mother to say another word. But even if Davy's sister was very ill, that was no excuse for running home from school without a word. There must be another reason. Guto wondered whether he felt jealous because the other lads hadn't chosen him as their leader. No, that couldn't be true, because they had both been the best of friends until very recently. What on earth could be wrong?

Chapter 13

Since the reopening of the school after the Midsummer holidays, the attendance is very considerably lowered. A great number of children have been withdrawn, and no reasons are given by the parents — but it has leaked out that they do not desire their children to mix with the children of 'traitors', meaning the children of quarrymen who have resumed work at the quarries. Several children have left for Tregarth, on account of the illtreatment meted out to them in this village.

(Llanllechid National School log book – 20 December, 1901)

What a disappointment! When Guto and his mother arrived in chapel next morning, there was no sign of Davy. As their family pews were right behind one another, he was hoping to see him at last and persuade him to talk things over on the way home after the service. But the pew behind was empty and not one of the family came that morning. Guto knew better than to ask his mother if he could go to see him on a Sunday, she would make sure that he stayed indoors and went to chapel three times. No playing outside, nor indoors either. He would have to learn a verse from the Bible to recite at the evening service and knew from bitter experience that she was sure to choose an extra long one to keep him busy all day.

The pew was still empty when he arrived for the six o'clock service. Then, as they all stood to sing the first hymn, he could sense some movement behind him and knew that they had arrived at last. He took a quick look as he sat down again for the reading, to see Davy and his parents sitting there

looking very worried. Sally must be worse, he thought. But what on earth are they all doing here then?

There was no preacher that evening, only a prayer meeting. He usually enjoyed the change, especially when Davy nudged him to try to make him laugh. This happened every time Richard Davies started on his round from the Big Seat to take the collection, his Sunday boots squeaking at every step. But when he stood up that evening there was no sign from Davy. Then, when Hugh Hughes began to pray, Guto took a quick glance over his shoulder. They always competed with each other, trying to count how many times he said 'Oh, Lord' during his prayer and then arguing about it all the way home. But tonight Davy took no notice of him, he just kept staring straight ahead as if he was in a trance.

Guto leaned forward, resting his forehead on the narrow shelf in front of him and pushing his fingers through one of the small, round holes which held the Communion glasses. He started to count, but found it hard to concentrate when he had so much on his mind. Then he became aware of a strange stillness all around him and decided to listen more carefully to the old man's words.

'Oh, Lord, there are those in your House tonight who have betrayed us all. Traitors, Oh, Lord, they have turned their backs upon us and upon you, Oh,

Lord. Give them the strength and wisdom to see the error of their ways, Oh, Lord...'

Then he heard a movement behind him, but as he tried to turn his head his mother grabbed his arm to stop him. When the long prayer eventually came to an end he did manage to take a quick look, but the pew was empty. The three of them had walked out in the middle of the service! He turned to his mother with a puzzled look on his face and then the truth suddenly dawned on him. 'Betrayed' and 'traitors' – those were the words that had caused such a stir. Did that mean that Davy's father had turned traitor?

Never! But that would explain his friend's strange behaviour lately, and in a way it gave him some comfort. At least he knew that he wasn't to blame. His mind wandered back to the happy times they had enjoyed that autumn, teasing the traitors' children and hooting at their fathers as they came home from the quarry. What would happen now, he wondered? It wouldn't be any fun without Davy, and his father would have to pass their house every day to go to work. Would the women hoot at him too? As he walked home from chapel on that cold, dark night, he felt as if the whole world had turned upside down.

★　★　★

His mother did her best to comfort him as they ate their supper that evening.

'You mustn't blame Davy or his father,' she said sadly. 'He had no choice, you know, when Sally is so ill. He knows that if he can earn a decent wage she's sure to get better, especially now that they can get her into hospital. It's so difficult for people to live and it seems to be getting worse. What will become of us, God only knows.'

'But they all get money from the strike fund, Mam. And there are three choirs travelling all over the country to raise more money. They've sent hundreds of pounds home already, haven't they?'

'Yes,' his mother agreed. 'But it isn't half enough. Now you remember to take good care of Davy in school tomorrow.'

School! Of course, he would have to face Davy in the morning, unless his parents had decided to move him to the Church school. Oh, no! He couldn't bear to think of his friend being illtreated, or having to mix with Robat and his cronies. He knew that the bully would be only too glad of the chance to get his own back. Unfortunately, he also knew that the others would expect him to treat Davy as he did all the other traitors' children if he wanted to keep on being their leader. Oh, life was hard!

Chapter 14

*The bad feeling caused by the Strike
caused some half dozen children to remove to
the Church Schools. I am gratified to find
that, with one exception, the children of
Strikers and Secessionists fraternize
together.*

*I have repeatedly warned the children that
I will not tolerate any molesting and they
seem to have acted accordingly.*

(Carneddi British School log book – 2 September, 1903)

By next morning the news had spread like wildfire.
Davy's father back at work! Guto felt very strange
walking down the hill by himself to school, but he
wasn't going to wait for Davy. He couldn't face his
old friend today of all days, they had both been so
keen to punish the traitors and their families from
the very beginning. He wasn't keen to see the other
boys either, but a crowd of them were waiting for
him by the school gates.

'Hey, have you heard?'

'Davy's father went back to the quarry this morning.'

'It's true, then?'

'Oh, yes. I saw him walking past our house.'

'I wonder if Davy'll come to school today?'

'No way. He'll move to Llan Church school, you'll see.'

'Best place for him, with all the other traitors.'

'Good riddance too.'

'We'll give him a good hiding when we get hold of him, won't we Guto?'

Guto stood there, listening to the others going on and on. Yes, those had been his very words so often in the past. After all, no-one had a right to break the strike when everyone else was suffering so much. Not even Davy's father.

'Well, what do you say, Guto? Shall we look for him after school? To show him what we think of him and his family?'

Everyone turned to face him, waiting eagerly for an answer. He knew that this was a test and that one of the others would soon take his place if he let them down now.

'Yes,' he agreed at last, trying to forget his own feelings and do what was right. 'Yes, that's what we'll do, lads. We'll show him!'

★ ★ ★

No-one expected to see Davy in school that morning, but he sneaked in when everyone else had gone to their places. Guto made a point of sliding away from him down the bench, to leave a space between them. Although he tried to keep his head down and get on with his own work, it wasn't easy. After all, they had been such close friends ever since they started in the Infants class. Although he kept reminding himself that every traitor deserved the same treatment, he knew deep down that there was a world of difference between Davy and Robat. Because of this he daren't even glance across at his old friend, in case he started feeing sorry for him. But he was very conscious of him sitting a few feet away, working quietly without a word to anyone. The morning seemed endless, but Guto dreaded playtime even more because he knew what was coming.

When Mr. Pugh released them at last, he kept Davy behind to go over his sums. That old fox knows which way the wind is blowing, thought Guto as he followed the other boys to the far end of the yard.

'Do you think Pugh knows what's going on?'

'Yes, bound to.'

'But he can't keep him in for ever.'

'He'll have to let him out sooner or later.'

'We'll be ready for him, won't we boys?'

'Oh, yes! Just you wait, Davy bach!'

'You've got it coming!'

'We'll make sure he never sets foot in our school again.'

'Llan school is the place for him, with all the other traitors.'

'Keep an eye on the door, lads. Then we'll be ready for him when he comes out.'

Guto listened to the others going on and on. Ben's voice was the loudest, as if he sensed how uncertain Guto was about the whole business. But he'd have to go along with them if he hoped to keep his place in the gang and for that very reason he felt cross with Davy for turning his back on him, instead of sharing his troubles. But then he thought, how would he himself have felt if Wil and Llew had turned traitors? He would have been too ashamed to face anyone, especially now that there was so much bad feeling in the village. But there was no excuse for breaking the strike, he kept reminding himself, and Davy must know that they had no choice but to punish him.

Luckily, Mr. Pugh came out to ring the bell and still no sign of Davy. Everyone ran to their lines, waiting for the command to march to their classes. Another hour to suffer, thought Guto, dreading having to sit so close to Davy again and ignoring him completely. Then he caught a glimpse of him, sneaking out through the door and running to the lavatories at the back of the building. A murmur went through the ranks and some of the older boys began to hiss.

'Silence! Who made that abominable noise?'

They all looked straight ahead, but no-one said a word.

'Now I warn you, boys. You can stand here until dinner time if that's the way you behave towards your fellow pupils. I've told you again and again that I won't tolerate any bad feeling in this school, whatever goes on in the village these days. And you know very well what will happen if you break that rule,' he added, looking straight at Guto.

'We'll get him at dinner time,' whispered Ben. Guto nodded, but his heart was in his boots.

★ ★ ★

When dinner time came Davy had to leave the safety of the classroom at last. The other boys had gone round the corner to hide behind the chapel wall, keeping well away from Mr. Pugh's eagle eye. When Davy eventually appeared they pushed him against the wall and two of the bigger boys held him. Everyone turned to Guto to see what would happen next. As he stood there he could sense the fear in Davy's eyes and knew exactly how he must be suffering. He could remember only too well how he himself used to feel when he had to face Robat and his gang. Then he thought how lucky he'd been, always having Davy there to defend him. He stood there for a long time, ignoring the angry cries urging him on.

'Go on, do something,' shouted Ben impatiently. 'If you haven't got the guts, I'll do the job for you with pleasure.'

Guto walked forwards slowly, still uncertain what to do. Then, when Davy turned his head to the wall expecting the first blow, he was shocked that his old friend was now afraid of him. He went up to him, stood resolutely by his side, put his arm around his shoulders and faced the others.

'Leave him be! He doesn't deserve all this. Don't you worry, Davy, I'm here to look after you.'

What happened afterwards...

The Great Strike, the longest in history, lasted for three years. Although people all over Britain supported the quarrymen and their families in their struggle, they were forced to go back to work on 14 November 1903, on Lord Penrhyn's terms. By then many young people had left the district and others failed to get their jobs back. A thousand men never returned to work in the Quarry and families were split up as many moved to work in other parts of Britain or emigrated to America. The people of Bethesda still remember the Great Strike and the way it affected the whole community for many years to come.